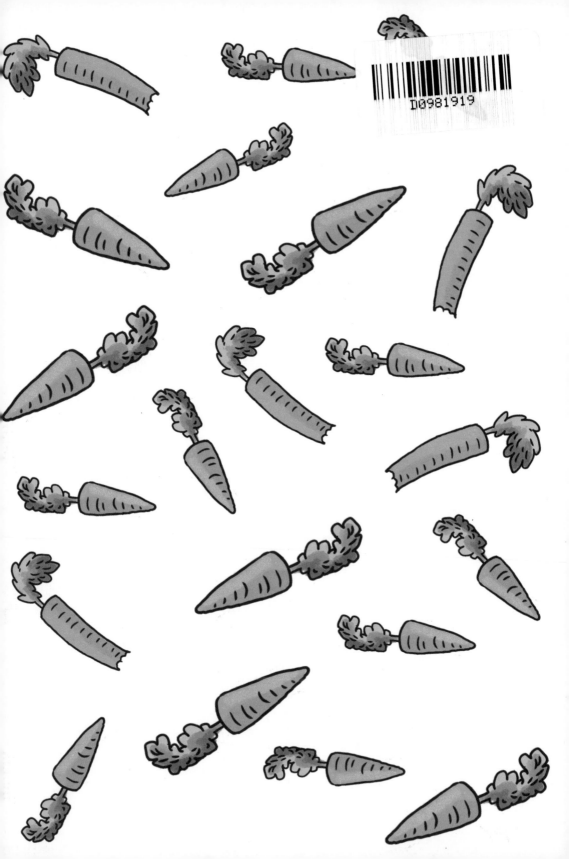

D0981919

Text copyright © 2024 by Marilyn Sadler

Cover art and interior illustrations copyright © 2024 by Roger Bollen

Cover art and interior illustrations by Tim Bowers

All rights reserved. Published in the United States by Random House Children's Books, a division of Penguin Random House LLC, New York.

Random House and the colophon and Beginner Books and colophon are registered trademarks of Penguin Random House LLC. The Cat in the Hat logo ® and © Dr. Seuss Enterprises, L.P. 1957, renewed 1986. All rights reserved.

Visit us on the Web!
rhcbooks.com

Educators and librarians, for a variety of teaching tools, visit us at RHTeachersLibrarians.com

Library of Congress Cataloging-in-Publication Data is available upon request.
ISBN 978-0-593-48033-5 (trade) — ISBN 978-0-593-48034-2 (library binding) —
ISBN 978-0-593-48035-9 (ebook)

MANUFACTURED IN CHINA
10 9 8 7 6 5 4 3 2 1

First Edition

Random House Children's Books supports the First Amendment and celebrates the right to read.

Penguin Random House LLC supports copyright. Copyright fuels creativity, encourages diverse voices, promotes free speech, and creates a vibrant culture. Thank you for buying an authorized edition of this book and for complying with copyright laws by not reproducing, scanning, or distributing any part in any form without permission. You are supporting writers and allowing Penguin Random House to publish books for every reader.

Bunny with a Big Heart

by Marilyn Sadler

illustrated by Tim Bowers

based on characters originally illustrated by Roger Bollen

BEGINNER BOOKS ®
A Division of Random House

P. J. Funnybunny
was a very busy bunny.
He was always
doing something.

"I'm going to the park!"
he shouted one morning.
Then he raced out of the house,
leaving the door wide open!

P.J. also left his dirty dishes

on the table . . .

. . . his toys all over
his bedroom floor . . .

. . . and Ritchie Raccoon's
baseball mitt under his bed!

"Sorry I'm late!" said P.J.
when he got to the park.
But P.J. was always late.

"Where's my baseball mitt?"
asked Ritchie.
"I'll bring it tomorrow," said P.J.
But that was what P.J.
said yesterday.

That night, Honey Bunny asked P.J.
to watch a movie with her.
"It's the new Hoppy Bunny movie!"
she cried.

But P.J. did not want to watch it.
"Those movies are for babies,"
he said.

P.J. thought only of himself.
He was too busy to think
of his family and friends!

Then one day, P.J. twisted his ankle sliding into second base!

"Ouch! Ouch! Ouch!" cried P.J.
as Ritchie and Potts
carried him home.

"My poor little bunny!"
said his mom.
"Keep your ankle up and rest!"
said his dad.

But P.J. did not want to rest.
He wanted to go
to Pine Coney Island
with his friends.

That afternoon, P.J.'s friends
came over with video games.
"Aren't you going
to Pine Coney Island?" P.J. asked.

But P.J.'s friends wanted
to stay and play with him.
"Pine Coney Island wouldn't
be fun without you," they said.

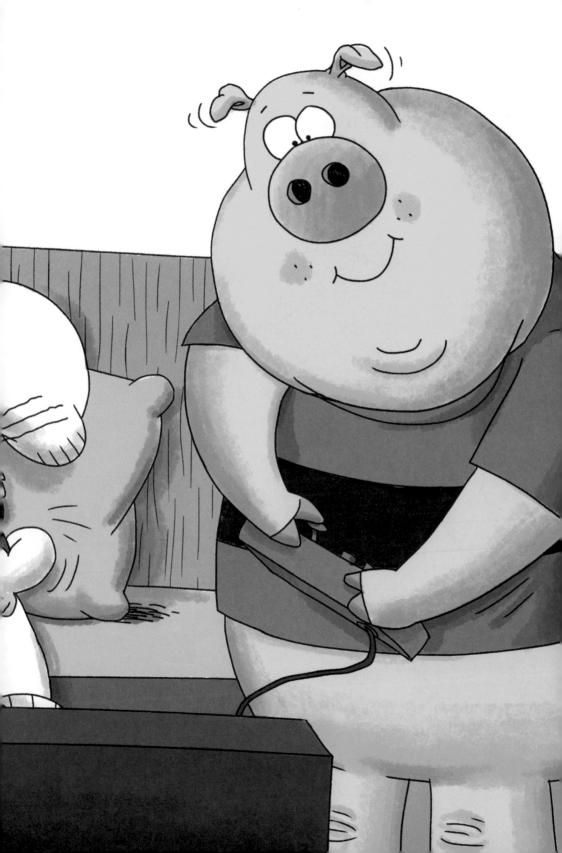

That night, P.J.'s mom
brought him dinner in bed.
It was macaroni and cheese.
P.J.'s favorite!

And when P.J. was ready for dessert,
Honey Bunny brought him carrot cake.

After dinner, P.J.'s mom
put a warm blanket over him.
And Honey Bunny
fluffed up his pillow.

Then his dad read him
a James Bunny book.

Everyone fussed over P.J.
the next day, too.

That night, P.J. thought about
all the kind things everyone
had done for him.
He was a lucky bunny.
But it was time for him to be
a more thoughtful bunny, too.

The next day,
P.J.'s ankle was better!
So P.J. made his bed.
Then he swept up all the
popcorn on the floor.

"We missed you, P.J.!"
said his family
when he sat down
for breakfast.

After breakfast, P.J. carried
everyone's dishes to the sink.

Then P.J. went to the park
to play with his friends.

"Sorry we're late!"
said Ritchie and Potts.
But Ritchie and Potts
were not late.
"I was early!" said P.J.
as he gave Ritchie his
baseball mitt.

That afternoon, P.J. returned
all of Ritchie's toys.
"I forgot you had my science kit!"
said Ritchie.

Then P.J. returned all of Potts's toys.
"I wondered where
my pogo stick was!" said Potts.

P.J. was happy. It felt good
to think of others!

That night, P.J. and Honey Bunny
watched one Hoppy Bunny movie
after another
after another
after another . . .

. . . until there were no Hoppy
Bunny movies left to watch!

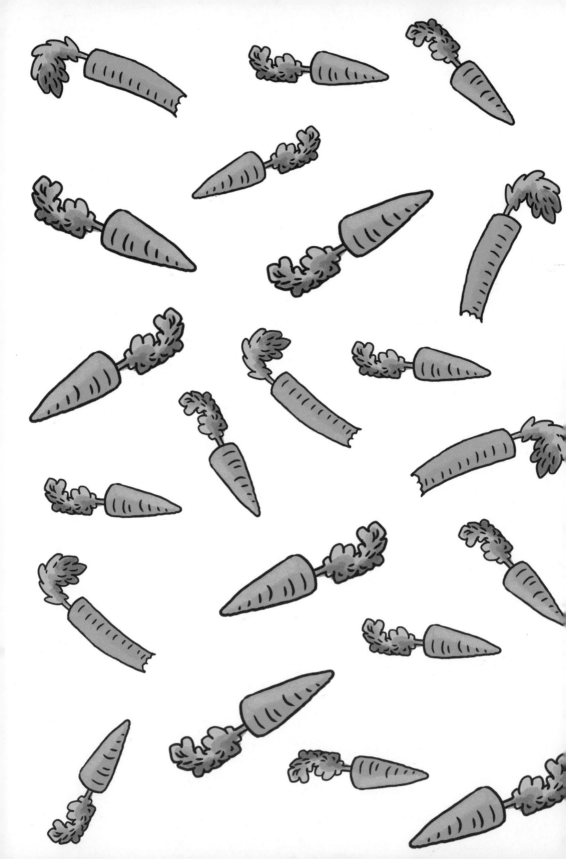